D0044151

Dear Parent:

Congratulations! Your child is taking the first steps on an exciting journey. The destination? Independent reading!

STEP INTO READING® will help your child get there. The program offers five steps to reading success. Each step includes fun stories and colorful art. There are also Step into Reading Sticker Books, Step into Reading Math Readers, Step into Reading Phonics Readers, Step into Reading Write-In Readers, and Step into Reading Phonics Boxed Sets—a complete literacy program with something to interest every child.

Learning to Read, Step by Step!

Ready to Read Preschool–Kindergarten
• big type and easy words • rhyme and rhythm • picture clues
For children who know the alphabet and are eager to begin reading.

Reading with Help Preschool–Grade 1
• basic vocabulary • short sentences • simple stories
For children who recognize familiar words and sound out new words with help.

Reading on Your Own Grades 1–3
• engaging characters • easy-to-follow plots • popular topics
For children who are ready to read on their own.

Reading Paragraphs Grades 2–3
• challenging vocabulary • short paragraphs • exciting stories
For newly independent readers who read simple sentences with confidence.

Ready for Chapters Grades 2–4
• chapters • longer paragraphs • full-color art
For children who want to take the plunge into chapter books but still like colorful pictures.

STEP INTO READING® is designed to give every child a successful reading experience. The grade levels are only guides. Children can progress through the steps at their own speed, developing confidence in their reading, no matter what their grade.

Remember, a lifetime love of reading starts with a single step!

Published in the United States by Random House Children's Books, a division of Random House, Inc., New York. Text originally published in a different form by Golden Books, an imprint of Random House Children's Books, a division of Random House, Inc., New York, in 1954.

Visit us on the Web!
StepIntoReading.com
randomhouse.com/kids

Educators and librarians, for a variety of teaching tools, visit us at
RHTeachersLibrarians.com

Library of Congress Cataloging-in-Publication Data
Brown, Margaret Wise.
I like fish / by Margaret Wise Brown, the author of Goodnight Moon ; illustrated by G. Brian Karas.
pages cm. — (Step into reading. A step 1 reader)
"Originally published in slightly different form by Golden Books, an imprint of Random House"—Copyright page.
Summary: In brief rhyming text, lists all the types of fish the narrator likes.
ISBN 978-0-385-36996-1 (trade pbk.) — ISBN 978-0-375-97178-5 (lib. bdg.) —
ISBN 978-0-375-98163-0 (ebook)
[1. Stories in rhyme. 2. Fishes—Fiction.] I. Karas, G. Brian, illustrator. II. Title.
PZ8.3.B815Ilf 2014 [E]—dc23 2012046758

Printed in the United States of America
10 9 8 7 6 5 4 3 2 1

STEP INTO READING®

I Like Fish

A STICKER BOOK

by Margaret Wise Brown
author of *Goodnight Moon*

illustrated by G. Brian Karas

Random House New York

Silver fish.

Gold fish.

Black fish.

Old fish.

Young fish.

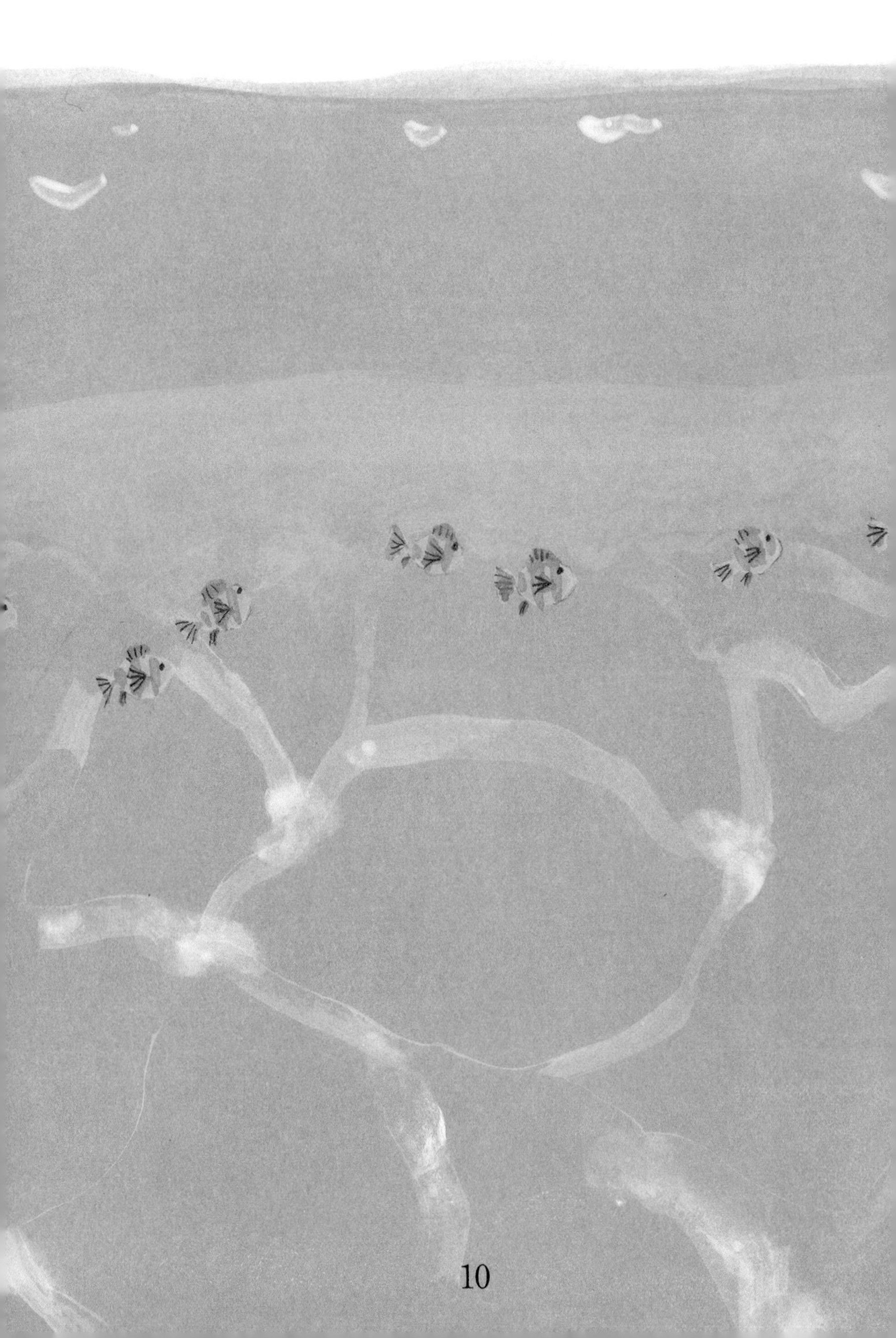

Fishy fish.

Any kind of fish.

A fish in a pond.

A fish in a stream.

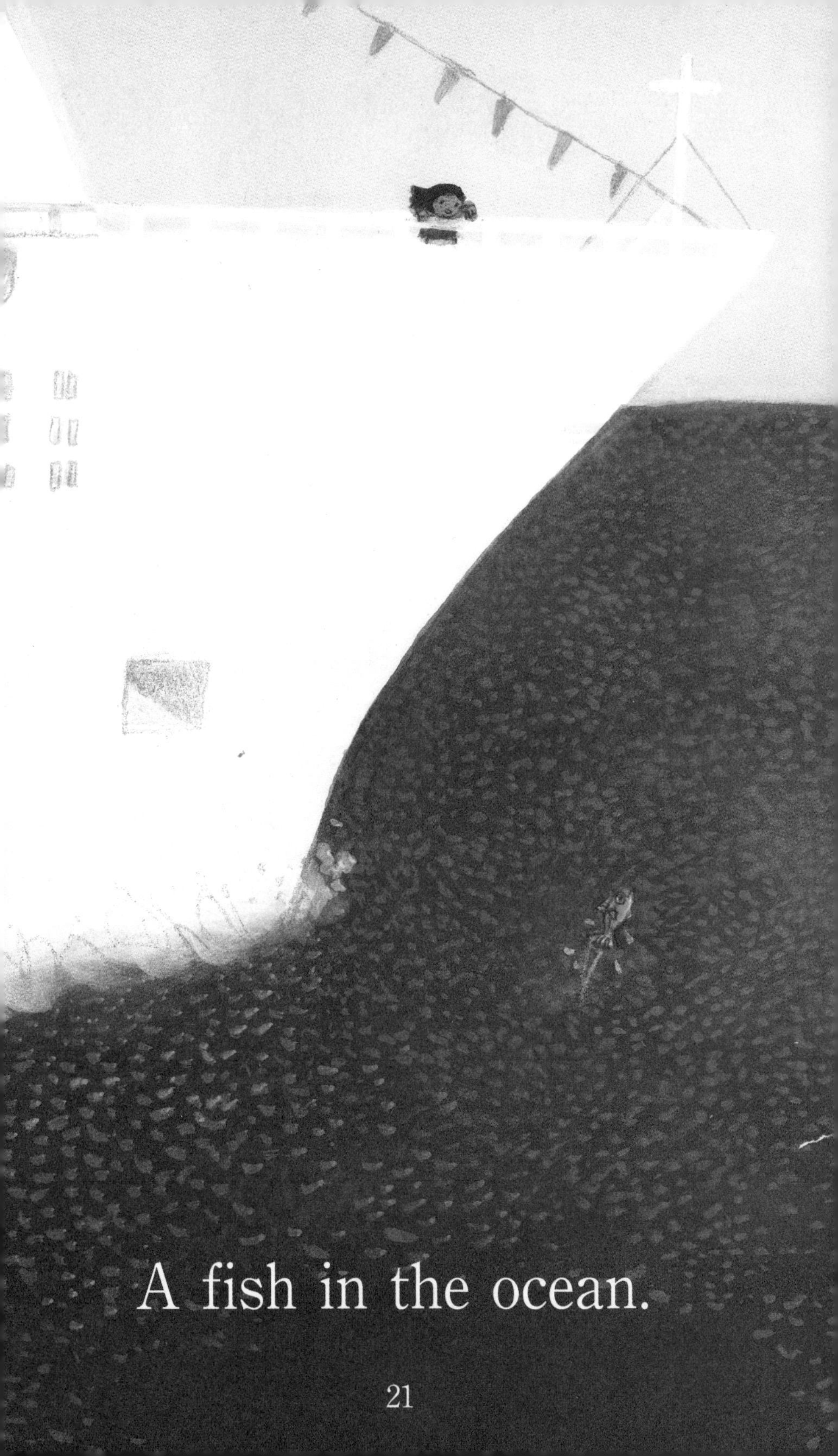

A fish in the ocean.

A fish in a dream.

I like fish.